~~ the way the tiger walked ~~

the way the tiger walked

by Doris J. Chaconas ～ Pictures by Frank Bozzo

Simon and Schuster, New York

To Michael
  because he is a tiger...
To Nick
  because he is a lamb...
And to Paula with the pumpkin cheeks

A tiger went for a walk in the jungle.
The fur on his back was smooth and rich,
as golden as a kingly crown, as black
as a raven's wing. There wasn't a sound,
the way the tiger walked.

   Under a jungle fern, a porcupine
walked with a waddle and a bump.
The quills on his back pointed straight
to the sky. His nose almost touched
the ground.

The porcupine watched the tiger walk.
He saw the tiger's golden coat,
velvety, thick and soft.

"How beautifully the tiger walks,"
the porcupine thought.

And because he wanted to be
beautiful, too, the porcupine laid down
his quills until they seemed velvety
smooth. Then, following the tiger — but
not too closely — he walked the way the
tiger walked.

The tiger heard a noise behind him.
Waddle-bump! Waddle-bump! The tiger
didn't stop. He didn't turn around. But
he smiled a little tiger smile.

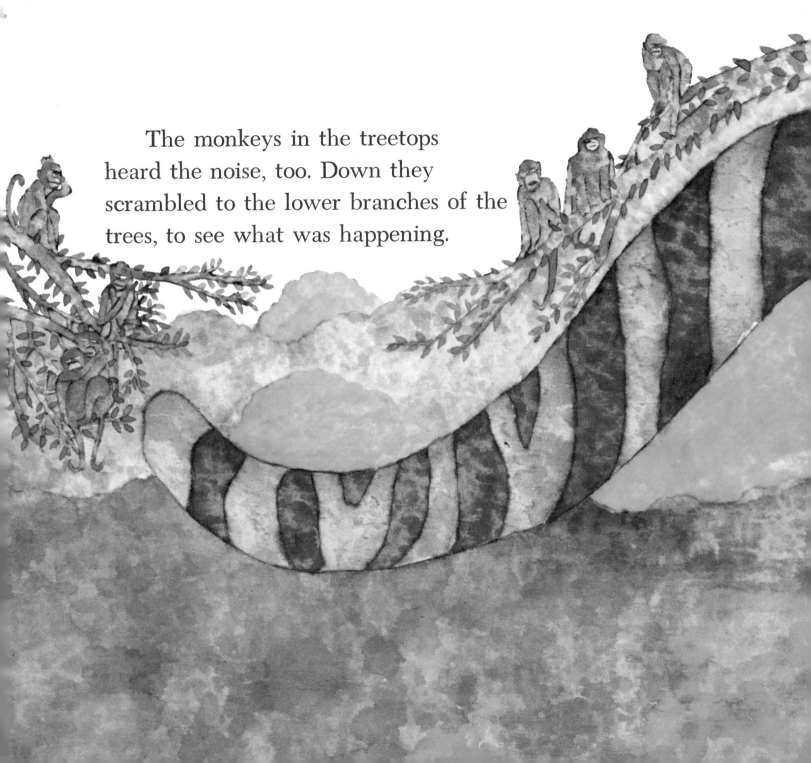

The monkeys in the treetops heard the noise, too. Down they scrambled to the lower branches of the trees, to see what was happening.

The tiger found a carpet of cool, green moss. He rubbed his back in the moss, waggling and wiggling his feet in the air.

The porcupine rolled on his back, too. But his long, sharp quills sank into the moss. He twitched and he twisted, but he was stuck. His short legs wiggled.

The monkeys giggled. But hand in hand, and tail in tail, hanging from the tree, they pulled the porcupine from the moss.

Underneath a jungle tree, a zebra
pranced with a clatter and a stomp.
He watched the tiger passing by.
He saw the tiger's muscles roll
beneath his golden fur.

"How gracefully the tiger walks," the zebra thought. He wanted to be graceful, too. So he tightened the muscles in his legs until they seemed as hard and smooth as stone. Then, following the porcupine, who was following the tiger — but not too closely — he walked the way the tiger walked.

Now the tiger heard two noises behind him. Waddle-bump! Clatter-stomp! The tiger didn't stop. But he grinned a secret tiger grin.

Then the monkeys saw the tiger swing his long tail, back and forth, sweeping and swooshing, until he caught it in his teeth.

The porcupine tried to catch his own tail. He squealed when the sharp quills stung his nose.

The zebra tried to catch his tail. Swinging his head far around to his side, he snorted as his bristly tail slapped him on the chin.

The monkeys laughed. One baby
monkey bit his own tail and cried.

An elephant in the thick jungle brush
walked with a rumble and a sway.
His ears flared out like large gray wings.
The earth shook under his heavy feet.
The elephant watched the tiger pass.

The tiger's stately head swung
back and forth slowly as he walked.
"How powerfully the tiger walks,"
the elephant thought. And because he
wanted to be powerful, too, he swung
his head as the tiger did. And, following
the zebra, who was following the
porcupine, who was following the tiger
—but not too closely—he walked
the way the tiger walked.

This time the tiger heard three noises behind him. Waddle-bump! Clatter-stomp! Rumble-sway!

The tiger crouched very low. As he walked, his stomach almost touched the ground.

The porcupine tried to walk in a crouch. But his legs were too fat. His legs were too short. They crumpled under him and he fell into the bushes.

The zebra laughed at the porcupine.
But when he tried to walk in a crouch,
he couldn't. His legs were too long.
They were too stiff. He fell back and
sat on his tail.

The elephant laughed at the zebra.
But when the elephant tried to walk in
a crouch, the jungle grass tickled his
belly. He toppled over with a
thunderous crash.

The monkeys laughed at them all.
They chattered and danced. This time
the baby monkey bit another monkey's
tail.

And then the tiger stopped.
He yawned a very great yawn.
He turned around.
The monkeys held on to their tails,
waiting to see what would happen.

The tiger crept slowly toward the other animals. When he came up to the porcupine, he suddenly ruffled up the fur on his black-and-golden back.

Each hair pointed straight to the sky. He walked with his nose almost touching the ground. Waddle-bump! Waddle-bump!

The porcupine sat on his tail in surprise. "What a beautiful way to walk!" he thought.

He shook out his quills. Then, looking like a thistle burr, he walked back toward his jungle ferns. And he walked the way a porcupine walked, with a waddle and a bump. Waddle-bump!

The tiger glided up to the zebra.
Then all at once the tiger arched his
neck. His feet danced quickly up and
down. Clatter-stomp! Clatter-stomp!

The zebra snorted with surprise.
"What a graceful way to walk!" he
thought.

And so the zebra shook out his stone-stiff legs. He pranced away, to find his jungle tree. And he walked the way a zebra walked, with a clatter and a stomp. Clatter-stomp!

The tiger stalked up to the elephant.
Then, suddenly, he spread out his ears
until they looked like small golden wings.
He walked with heavy steps, and
the ground shook under his feet.
Rumble-sway! Rumble-sway!

The elephant's trunk curled up in surprise. "What a powerful way to walk!" he thought.

And then the elephant slowly raised his head. He held his trunk up high. He trampled back to his jungle brush, walking the way an elephant walked, with a rumble and a sway. Rumble-sway!

The monkeys had been quiet long enough. They chattered and screamed, and they scolded the tiger for spoiling the fun.

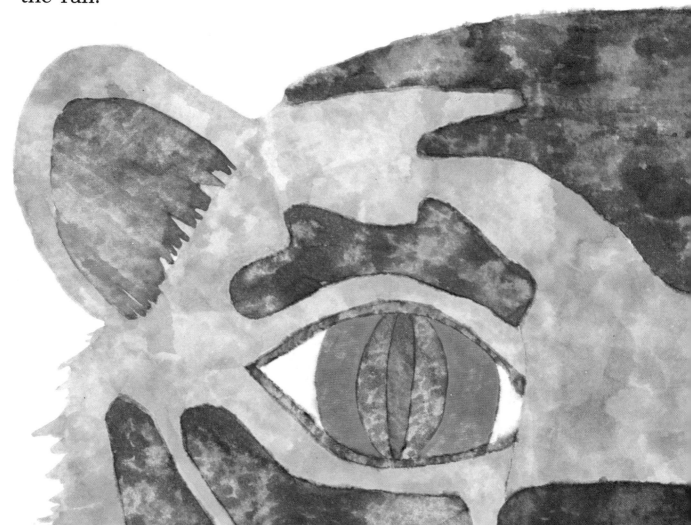

The tiger looked up into the trees.
He opened his mouth, showing all of his
great white teeth, and then he filled the
air with a terrible, thundering roar:
ARRRRH!

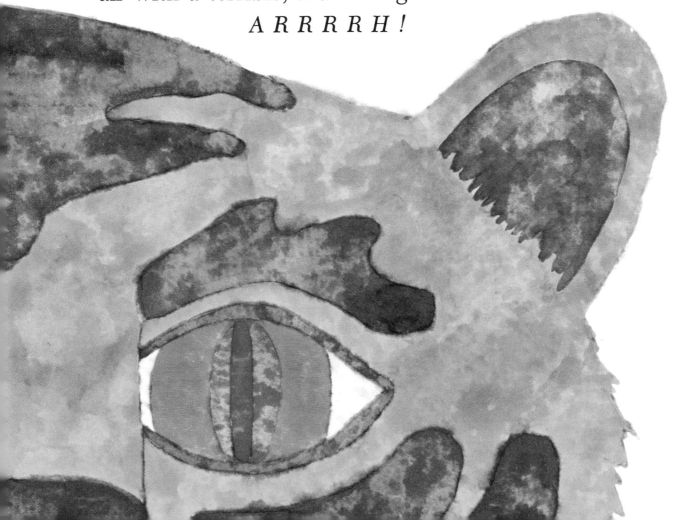

The monkeys clamped their hands over their mouths and didn't make another sound.

The tiger finished his walk in the
jungle. He smiled a knowing tiger smile.
And there wasn't a sound,
the way the tiger walked.